with only
which she could carry

a poetry collection

by

Nicole Jean Turner

Hardcover Edition. Published by the Underground Writers Association of Portland, Maine. Set in Garamond typeface.

NicoleJeanTurner.com

ISBN: 978-0-578-81156-7

Nicole Jean Turner is an artist from New England with an affinity for vignettes, napping outdoors, and conversations that confront the human condition. She writes in cursive to hide the butchered spelling that would otherwise raise suspicion about her master's degree in writing. Turner has published individual pieces of poetry, prose, and visual art in anthologies and journals every year since 2012. She crowd-funded one limited run chapbook, *Coffee Stout and Rain Water* in 2017. This is Turner's first full length poetry collection. Read her latest at, NJTPoetry.com.

CONTENTS

Climb; alternate cover
by Hal Goucher

With Only Which She Could Carry is a collection of poems chronicling transient characters trying to establish lives in multiple spaces at the same time, existing everywhere and nowhere at once. The author invites you to read, consider, and imagine a life lived out of terminals, stations, and the ether. Consider the motions of a life pressed through these turnstiles and what shapes might be formed of you from it. Consider what you might take and leave behind.

DEDICATION

to Jean and Bruce

for consistently being a phone call away from, wherever I've run

ACKNOWLEDGMENTS

*To those who have provided couches and blankets when airlines left me stranded,
when bars and bus lines shut down for the night, or when I was simply in town, this collection
exists thanks to you and your inexorable support despite the vicissitudes and distance.*

If You Should Fall Lost

Toss me back into the rose water.
I want to float down the river
on my back, wrapped in garlands
of chartreuse and conifer cone
like a Viking's cuirass hand fashioned from the forest
to embrace the body, shelter the shoulder sewn heart;
mine rocks in tune with the riverbank lapping,
my bones can feel the rudder vibrations pulling
trade winds are tugging these sails North West
while I'm strung out on Jack, telling all of my Kates,
I'm no longer a man of science
give me faith
give me fate
give me the city where my feet move
like cherry blossoms in April winds
and Mama Cass Elliot takes my hand
dancing up the sidewalk
every mile until I'm in
the home I hand fashioned,
from roses and thorns.

The Astronaut

This is the third interstellar bar this week.
On a pioneer's never finished journey,
a neon hall behind a blue reflection;
he's drinking an oil slick again.

This is just another surface to sit, take off the helmet for a bit,
strain the lungs on some fresh thin air, here, we find the astronaut
in his natural habitat. A pit stop
somewhere on the way to sector whatever
the destination never matters.
He won't be staying long.

He gets high on the atmosphere and strung out on change,
he hangs at the rail just long enough
to be overwhelmed by epinephrine
endorphins, the closest thing he can remember
to how it felt to be warm without the suit.

This astronaut, he drinks black ice and chews lime tonic,
befriends for the night the same type of Martian
from the space bar before, always some regular.
He's jealous of their commitments, telling them,
how lucky to have a name and be wanted
in the place they're most comfortable and understood.

This astronaut, he lives a dream,
charts unseen galaxies,

but can't find the gravity to stay or say;

how sad the heart that beats

thick and full in a body by itself.

He carries on into the glitter searching

for a black hole to fall into, or someone

                          with more

than just a spare oxygen tank, someone

who'll look at him the way Galileo looked to the moon.

Disconnect

When you're wayward, they don't see you
long enough to notice
the inches in growth.

                                        You're alone with your evolution
                                              on whatever locomotive
                                        you've chosen this go around.

Every city has lights but
none of them stay on late enough.
                        This sort of limbo incites
                        a loneliness best described
                        by a time-zone that doesn't exist
                        a plane in the ether
                        between longing and excitement
a dream state which can so easily become a nightmare
                        they say microbes in the gut cause it, drive the brain wild
                but whatever causes a body to lose its circadian rhythm
is not so easily grounded back in reality by a healthy diet.
                                                            A wayfarer
                        can see the rivers below their airplane are flowing
                but can't feel the motion of any body of water other than their own.
the word home becomes a foreign concept
emotional bonds melt all sun blocked
                        we call these cosmoses liminal
                        we call ourselves limitless

Gold Medalist

How many times have I called myself hopeless
romantic on a dating app, to a stranger across a sticky table
somehow unable to admit I'm more than full
of hope for every interaction had, tell them these things tend to last
when you filter them more than your photos and responses
just jump past the endearing falsehoods about how well together ones life is
get right to it the big questions, the can you handle confrontation
I'm tired of talking tiny details into topics
we've both rephrased to a dozen other temporary partners
favorite colors middle names and would you what ifs
I want to know what you believe in.
Are you going to play coy when I ask about building seven
or will you take a moment to entertain my excitement
and maybe for just a second consider
confronting you preconceived notions
let me nit-pick the narrative they've given you
I want to know
if you're going to order that twelve ounce just to
get comfortable or if you know that the man who made it
fell in love with the art of brewing from the rogue hops growing
over the neighbor's garden, the whole of it;
Is it really so hopeless to find the romance
in making someone so suddenly seen
they shift in seat
then pushing past that passé
like the ice caps weren't melting and breaking ice was my Olympic sport
how are we ever to love each other if you won't

own your faults on the first damn date, baby give it to me.

The date I asked you on and left you stumbling around the answer

because it's not the demure nature of today's woman to be so forward online

or even in real life, we're all connected at so perfect a digital distance

that anyone doing their best to break that habit is considered hopeless.

I find it romantic. To stand for something

that thing being myself

the some being just enough attitude

I suppose the hopeless part is the stories I've made of all of them

and the pages no one will ever know they've inked

in their ancient game participation

The Salutatorian's Address

/ *"JUNE FIFTH: Portland Community Clown College News Bulletin: Due to unforeseen circumstances at last night's graduation, all classes have been canceled for today. Grief counseling and burn triage is available at McMenamins Crystal Hotel. May God have mercy on us all." –The final update ever made to the Portland Clown College website in 2010.* /

He graduated second in his class from a top tier clown college on the north west coast of the states. Somewhere far from the city he grew up in surrounded by acres of wildlife and woodlands; on graduation day he sat at a lake drinking moonshine mixed with maraschino cherries and slowly melting face paint. Walking the stage for a ceremonial pie face
felt like a waste of time. So he didn't go. He sat alone through the morrow.
He let the grimy sand of mountain lake edges wash into his red leather shoes while listening to a news report on a small flower shaped radio pinned to his suit.
Over his heart the broadcaster's words swam through the plastic speaker petals like snakes in the water he be before. Someone blew up a bank in desperation this morning.
Lost everything, took their life in one final display of panic, resignation.
In Pakistan, a bus turned over and killed at least a dozen. The wildfires consuming Siberia should soon reach permanent uninhabitable levels of pollution. There are also fires in Canada, California, and somewhere off a once charming hillside of Vancouver.
The graduate draws stick figures in the sand with a slimy stick.
Maraschino cherries burn the back of his tongue, when a child runs up on him. She points at his spry pink hair spiked in every direction, and with wide eyes reaches as if lifting herself to the sky to pull down a cloud worth napping on, the child's doe eyes melt into a whimsical smile as her interstellar fingers touch down. Gentle little carrots

wrinkled with chub growing faster than the bones beneath push his cheeks up
and flatten smile lines under her reach.

"Smile Mr. clown!"

The Portland wind rattled its way past the bog,

curtsied o'er the pines and hustled around the ferns.

"Are you sad

because it's too cold to swim?"

Her blissful innocence overwhelmed him.

She retracted her fingers, now sticky with paint, and planted them palm down
on the lakes edge. He watched storms of opaque ink sprawl over pebbles, an
army of acrylic soldiers forcing against the current to break free from her grasp,
tossed like paratroopers as she shook and splashed her hands. He heard them
screaming under heavy fire, felt the machine gun pops as droplets landed on
his pants, then realized the NPR reporter in his pin

had channeled to a correspondent live somewhere in central America. The
child turned from the water and stood in awe of the despondent man. His legs
stretched before him covered in speckles of sand, his arms in his lap, she
pondered for a moment then mirrored his image dropping to his side with
arms and legs slack.

"Do you tell any jokes?"

After a long pause

of the wind whistling up the path, the graduate pulled out his transcript from a
deep breast pocket and had a laugh.

"You're not a very funny clown, Mister. My—um—my favorite joke is, um—
ok let me tell you."

He pulled his legs up to a cross while the child rocked back and forth.

"What's—what's black, and white, and red, all over?"

The graduate thought of racial tensions in the city. Slaughtered animals at
poacher's hands. A newspaper, he sighed.

With glee the girl jumped from her cross-legged seat and exclaimed, *"a zebra with a sunburn!"*

Her pocket began to glow and jingle, and as if caught eating candy without permission, the girl opened the clamshell to her mother's beckon. She kissed the graduate's forehead like a honeybee greeting a flower, then scampered off down the bike trail behind them without a word or hesitation. From an inside a hidden pocket he drew a slew of tissue then fished out a banana yellow notebook. A spotted bookmark reserved a speech written for today that would never be heard. "We are gathered here today, he read aloud
to the undisturbed and abandoned lake with an orotund bitter palate, "to celebrate our uncanny ability to face these dark times with a smile on our face. Painted on daily, we as a whole are responsible for, liable by, servants of the greater good. Somewhere a frog croaks and a twig bends under the beast's chin. "The world out there expects us,

 this generation to make magic

while they drive axes into the stage.

We are not to complain of pain or sorrow

for any longer than it takes to turn it witty.

We are this world's last hope at salvation.

We are necessary.

The salutatorian laughs.

Tears the page, and bites into a soggy maraschino cherry.

Moving Mt. Tabor

At some corner I'll find the way.
In some shadow, under last season's
decay at the base of the mountain
I'll hum out the vibrations, a thousand
silent noises shivering to come out;
a thousand bubbles in my throat
trying to be thunder. Under one of these pines
I'll rearrange the muscles in my face,
contort and gnash tongue and teeth
to push this atmosphere between us
in such a way that you'd understand
the gravel below my collar, this fist
full of road is pumiced.
I may veer up a mulch trail and catch splinters
but I cling to the movement of cement fishnets
open and sprawling;
by always moving on I am in control
by always moving away
it's easier to find the highway
than arrange letters and curve my lips around
an ending we'll both like

School For The Deaf

We play a mind game across a lagoon of liquor
question and answer not so important more a
how does one react and respond and pull apart
type situation, something I haven't done in a while.

This fishbowl we call scorpion for the flaming center
is a quick ticket to drowning, and a life preserver
for awkward conversation. Opening up to strangers;
it's not lost on me how many writers bare all on page
but need the assistance of a substance to get it out
the mind game is a crutch the same as an ice pick
a proxy for connecting across a language barrier
as creative types speak best with their hands
and with a mouth full of scorpion bowl I'm doing my best
to interpret their lip shapes and sign back rudimentary
attempts at American Sign Language. I've made several
less than flattering grammatical errors in this place.

This language is less about the words, the movements
of the eyebrows and shoulders are so important
body language is where the subconscious sings loudest
the mind game is a sort of humming, a chatter vibration
teeth on the edge of truth, shared smiles are only the half of it.

We play nostalgia volley across the table with just a few years between us,
it's been so long since this space has heard our laughter the way it once did,
the way twenty-one-year-olds pretend to have any idea what they're doing,
we could go on for hours with the same twelve months of chaotic material.

I don't always come here to fall in love but when I do it smells like leftovers
and maybe that's the least romantic way to say some old friendships are still
hanging out somewhere in the back of the fridge just waiting for the trash
that I'm not ready to take out but here we are, in the same old vinyl booths
with a bottle of booze at the center of a table I've watched dead friends eat
off of with their nose and others pillow their overindulged foreheads on
this dining room will forever taste like a life lived before my own began

just a townie bar for a group of kids I so desperately wanted to fit in with
but didn't. I had to leave to understand out of sight out of mind is more
than a mind game of tired excuses. When talking to strangers is easier
than signing the truth in a familiar space to a familiar face I've known since
before I could talk with my hands and mouth at the same time, we let
the conversation fly off with dragonfly breaths of transparent wings

we let the reality of adults growing apart be. Question and answers not
so important more a how does one react and respond and pull apart
the nuances of closed posture and uncomfortable laughter filling lulls.

Does It Still Serve You

Cough drops and coffee, overdue on a good shower,
all intertwined aromas that don't bother the nose much
when you're bleeding,
being scooped off the floor by your vest,
two sausage hands hooked under your shoulders
                    God
reaching down into darkness,
a six-plus-foot leather wrapped giant pulls you to your feet
effortlessly, as if your frame were plush,
than a tap on the shoulder assures you're alright
and you're thrust back into the madness
blood and sweat streaked across your glasses
like a hunter, hungry, thrown back into the bush.

This is the angel of the pit.

I met him at fifteen years old and he has followed me
to every punk show since my first punch in the nose,
he stands beside me in dingy basements,
he hovers four steps back in crowded arenas;
I've stitched the sight of his eyes in the distance to my heart
like the patches on the biker jacket he adorns,
screen printed medals of war show what he's survived

outside of these walls on the street
in thirty minutes he will evaporate through the crowd
dispersed in the direction of cheap run-down parking
but he is not gone.

The angel of the pit
is he who makes rock shows a home.

this guy is the one you lock sight with
as you're crowd surfing and drop your shoe,
he's the comforting wall of human
that keeps overzealous swinging elbows away from you.

I've been to radio pop concerts
and country band dances
and never have I felt
as safe as I do when that titan is around.

The last time I was knocked out
from a hit to the base of my skull,
the angel of the pit carried me aside
and morphed back into the crowd
before I could open my eyes

to thank him.
I sat in the daze
and wondered if this space still served me
had it become merely a tomb to visit and grieve
where I knew I could find Him

a genuine human keeping us safe
in a sea of chaos.

The Astronaut II

The Astronaut moved
and then he moved back
and then he moved back and back

there's no forth in space just drifting
just weightless shapeshifting from system to system
and in each one someone asked him what was next
the ship outside dinged with a hundred parking spots to small for it

A song played; the Astronaut somehow connected to a radio wave
and thought, this sounds just like me, maybe I am still in reach of—
this melody these lyrics, I'm not alone out here after all—

The Astronaut tried to share his helmet
so others could understand him through the tune
but the wayfaring kind don't get much sympathy from
those who feel shackled to a station for good.

The Astronaut sings along, hums in the vacuum of nothingness
coasting through the ether either catching glimpses of
how this all could be real and worth it
or simply filling the void with leg tapping, finger snapping
a heart made less heavy by a simple tune.

Cross Country Again

They will ask why, and slowly your explanation
for leaving will grow shorter, fatigued from
feigning remorse, the word sorry starts to sound
foreign. You'll tell someone you want to spend a
year in Canada, someone else, that you're just
broke. It doesn't matter anymore why but when
how long is left to take in everything you'll
dream of on the other side of the airplane.
Returning is inevitable so regret for going now is
not there. They will ask how soon and say we
should even though we never did all those times
before you don't have to worry. The delicious
unknown of next has always been your favorite.
When they ask why and when and how long tell
them you'd rather be present for however long,
right now, because.

Hopeless Queer

I write a genderless love poem
about a material object and send a person into a panic,
it reads like a confession to infidelity and I now admit to the ambiguity
but the soul of a poem if nothing else is in the reader's own subconscious,
what they see in the words is an interpretation
of the verses they've been struggling to narrate themselves.
I do my best not to make assumptions from those reactions.
I write a genderless love poem
about a man I was hopelessly eyeing across a party and a girl
comes up to the stage afterward to ask me on a date because I speak so
beautifully about the women I've loved
and I don't know how to react. I thank them, because I try to.
But politely excuse myself. Mull over the word choices
and leave it alone. It's not often something I create
is read correctly the first time around.
I choose to write genderless more often than not with intent
not even for the sake of immersion
rather I've felt so fondly for genders on all dots of the spectrum
I've grown tired of explaining myself to anyone.
My sexuality is loving my gender is me
my existence is ambiguous at its core and I'm not sorry.
I can write with both hands;
I write an identity poem
using words like androgynous and fluid and more than one person
decides to tell me what I am afterward,
because that's how these things work now. One tells me
there's no discrimination anymore because gay marriage is settled,

and I don't know where to start.

I don't fight it anymore.

I can't control how I'm viewed anymore than I can how I'm liked

and I'd rather give my attention to writing my partner into love poems

than any concern

with if someone wants to label me into something simple to work with.

When asked I say queer

when asked further I say why

when my assertions are met with denial I shrug and suggest

reading a book once and a while might open

the appreciation that human nature

is to settle into duality rather than embark into unfamiliar

light and dark wrong and right

it simplifies our existence into something comfortable. Dual options.

I write a genderless self-love poem

that makes a crowd of people uncomfortable and I publish it in a book.

it reads like a confession to heartbreak that only one partner has ever said

they accept me as however I am

and I now admit the soul of an ambiguous poem if nothing else

is a desire to be taken without question.

To exist without the need for more.

Dog Ear'd Pages

I scrapbook and journal most of my moments
like little pennies in a swear jar on a ship headed north,
sea storms produce a lot more for memory than beach breeze
and I think there's a compass bearing stuck in me.
I wonder how sailors handle such ships, fishermen headed for king crab legs
tossed around through the worst waters they could sail
all for shellfish. All the mystery I've wailed over has been selfish
all things considered, hundreds of dollars have washed in and out of my wallet
for frivolities and tourist excursions all over this country.
I have more clipped tickets from this year
than some people have dinner options
and so often I'm still hung up on a heart jet lagged
off the travel between shining early in the east
and fading to black out west. I want to stay suspended,
I want to be a sunset that doesn't have to finish
setting. I set myself up for so many open-ended questions,
from casual hows things beens to particular stanza inquisitions
when I'm just trying to scrapbook. Just trying to finish this new book
and get it on the shelf, with a handful of page corners dog ear'd down
yoga posing my mistakes and most humbling moments of fragility
to go back and mull over some time else. Moments of wonder
where I've won or lost or just existed in some suspension between
every detail a little receipt, every comma a breath
gasping for pause in the constant changing I've assumed a life in.
I envy the sailors up in the Alaskan pacific. Taking a voyage
with a clear goal, dated finish, winds to follow lanes to stay in.

Thirteen hundred days is a lot of pages to log, interpreting the scribbles

in the margins left under the corner folds in these

marble mixed maidens' manuscript, it's imperfect.

It's a library book taken out a hundred times over, battered by mystery stains

and bookmarked corners, the folds, the damage to a page we cause

just to find where we left off because there is no maritime locator

for life like on the ocean,

all our remembering for whatever wears us

is weathered worse than any sea salt storm

that's battered down the oldest of rigs. Even the Titanic has a romanticized

place in history.

We're all guilty of it in our own way, hanging on to sentences

returning to phrases and maybe we unfold

an old corner or two before putting our books away

but the little wrinkle, the way smile lines crease a face into scarred happiness

our obsessive revisiting of misunderstandings and grievances leaves marks.

When I walk through the aisles of used bookstores

to seek out old copies of Moby Dick

bookmarked and worn out and passed in and out of hands

it didn't find a home in

I don't feel so much shame for my shambles,

I stop holding myself to some standard

no one else has ever lived. Misshapen edges

are part of the process of getting through some things.

Not every journey should be journaled only focused on the brilliance,

suns do cast shadows even on beaches.

I wrote this one love note, heart jetlagged on a draft I was leaving behind

because everything we've set in stone

seems only to be as strong as the ocean tides wearing off the edges.

And right then, I felt polished.

I'm still marking these moments to revisit, just like everyone else is I am
returning to things unfinished and unsure,
only now I'm taking time to enjoy the truth of things on all sides
I'm taking time to understand situations as more than their cover's appearance.

When All Else Fails

cover the walls in prints and paintings picked

up at the marker, walked along the greenway

and taken through the stone steps to the solitude

of a one-bedroom single occupancy

three thousand miles away from anybody

or thing you've ever known; you know art.

like the value of a repress limited run

how it isn't in the rarity. it's the partial grocery

trip it paid for, cost twice over already

to produce on a wish. a confidence

called passion. plaster the kitchen

with as many artisan items found

in walking distance. a car

cost about ninety-five livelihoods minimum,

you can walk the extra block to cover it.

you can watch the runners on the greenway

from your hand woven patio runner

and let that outsider syndrome imposter identity

consume or you can fill your life with passions on loan

from local crafters and get to know

the neighborhood through the vision

of persons inspired. get to know yourself again

anti-shopper pro-procurer

Does It Make A Sound

and not one of them said sorry

the fallen cherub repeated
a strange hang up, words
we want when wronged
a sort of ancient ransom
atone for these sins, like the fallen
deserves some sort of altar
worship in the ashes of trust to your martyr
as skies break and thunder calls
forth the wrath of some other Valhalla
...this is what pain does, it's not attractive.
robs the reasonable of peace, in place puts insecurity
eventually, it breeds an animal lust for retribution

the former winged one
really tries not to hold it against them.
the original actions that led all
to the final act and plot reveal
nobody enjoys an I told you so
and the universe tends to speak loud enough
on our behalf in time and truth
but
after years of shouting fears from sodden clouds,
brining reems of evidence to the court of public opinion
starting with small secrets and eventually full transcripts
and still cast the villain

still stuck in the clutches of having washed the feet of a monster

until another came forward to echo that hurt

and the reverberations caused pause to listen

to both of them. if a tree falls alone in the woods

the fallen takes a new form, looks back

at the textbook progression of traumatic

healing, as evidence to the contrary, wonders

does the cherub lack the charm of an abuser

so much so that women are still whispering in bathrooms on

how both the Shepard and lamb exaggerate the means of slaughter

or how he made it so easy to forget because the fallen was so dramatic

so easy to drown out the sound of a creature caring for its hurt alone

because the badger in the bear trap should have stopped going to the woods

if it really hurt that much. never mind its pack, its home.

and no not one of them said sorry.

an act of acknowledgment

that we were valid on our own

as a person as a servant to some ancient form,

assurance our part in the tragedy doesn't justify the fall

Model 1

Self-care is the scent of machine oil
The gentle pound of carbon on pounds of pressed fiber
Replacing ribbon in a hand wound model one
Self-care is forgiving the ink for staining everything you touch
It's a process, a manual effort to refurbish
Because even well-cherished collector's items need upkeep
And not just cosmetic
replacements for bent keys with no clear attachment point
Things that require manuals they stopped printing in 1938
will take time to sort out
The human is no different than a portable typewriter.
It will break down for no clear reason sometimes
It will need odd parts shipped in
Using it will damage it but you're not just going to shelf yourself
to preserve superficial beauty are you?
It will also need you to stop using that damn buzz word
like it's a mood, self-care
Taking care of yourself is so much more
than the reduction to a phrase it's become.
The two words associated with face masks and bubble baths
glass of wine perhaps

No

Real self-care is getting dirty and digging through everything that isn't working
until you find the bent pin jamming you up
It's taking stock of everything physical and mental that makes you happy or not
then deciding what goes out to the curb for Tuesday recycle pick up

and what gets added to the to-do list of salvageable.

An itemized attack plan.

A purchase list for the tinker shop.

A pile of tiny screw drivers and wrenches that could be for dolls

but for now will wind these hinges down

tighten up the roller.

Taking care of one's self is forgiveness for the mess you're going to make.

Taking care of one's self is learning how all the moving parts work together

and knowing when to call for an appointment with an authority on tinkering.

It's so much more than a poem.

It's taking a rusty Remington and giving it another 81 honest years of love

Onward

These dark chiseled woods and iron edgings,

fixings, this cafe has hosted my jitters dozens of

times. The quiet goodbye in revisiting spaces I

have loved dozens of evenings, reliving is a

traveling funeral. There is no clear path of

return, only the cold brew I'm taking in another

final now. Each breath single origin, poured over

the words and muscle memory focused on the

details. The yellow lamps, the hanging orbs of

glass cupping succulents. Folks tell me all these

coffee shops are the same and a waste of

money, my wallet smiles when opened. My

elbows hug the mahogany countertop the

record player hugs back. The blues, the bass,

the procession carries on until my heart cannot

take the extra beating.

Talking in Asclepias

I almost asked him on a date
to the poetry bar I used to frequent,
flirted with the beautiful thought.
I want to read something that'll make him blush
be flooded by the greenhouse gates opened up;
if the monarchs weren't going extinct, I'd trap one
from his laughter and give it to him preserved in pins.
I've been planting milkweed in the ditch of my palms for weeks to feed them.
I don't know how else to capture
the warm glow that flies when he talks
about that placement in the card tournament he got
or the way he leaned over the table to listen
when I talked about the new approach to writing I'm taking.
The restaurant became an arboretum
while we talked passions like teenagers share the flu;
I would give a month to bed-bound fever
if I could save the hue of his blush with my leftovers
from the moment he realized I was talking about him when I first said
beautiful.
I want to trade that sense of special for the moment of shy
whatever the exchange rate.
So I texted image attachments
of pens burst and ink stains, flirting up the courage to expose myself
in that old haunt. My morning paper and pour over
I've long since traded out for the drive over and drive through caffeine
switched from annual migration to perennial inhabitation

of his side of the world,

I hadn't even noticed the little changes I'd adopted

since their presence grew so naturally.

For years, I had read about him at that bar anonymously

I almost asked him there because

I just want to read something

that'll make him fall in love with the sound of his own name.

Like my voice were nectar, and the monarchs were hungry.

Iris Palmer and Her Suitcases

There's a woman in Vogue, 1977
struggling with a tower of luggage
at least that's the implication,
that she cannot carry it all alone.
A model and all of her revels, beauty boxed up
on to the next shoot caught in this postcard pose
faceless behind all that defines her cradled close,
somehow redefined as a symbol for detriment,
the mistake they say at every page turn
is to be too much, being alone is too much,
what is so wrong with Ms. Palmer doing the work for herself?
Who is the onlooker to say she isn't balancing this act just fine
on those six-inch baby doll heels, I see no waver in her posture.
I see no failure on the part of woman standing singular
carrying the tools of her trade and the weight of the world's judgement
successful is not packaged in petite frames on most store shelves
so to be captured by Vogue is a deviation from our expectations.
The male gaze of the photographer shooting is to be taken as deceptive,
where is the interpretation that he saw her for strength and determination
to carry it all
to be a woman in Vogue on her own
to chase a starlit dream with only which she could carry

Theorist

The universe sure has a funny way
of embodying what's on our minds without even asking.
Some call it manifesting, an art of bringing into focus
what is at the horizon of the mind
an iridescent glimmer stared at until its diamond
can be found outside of the meditation.
Some call it a coincidence, that a condition
of our reality is being unconscious until the obvious
grabs your attention, screams from its core
that this is here and now and so are you.
A weird shade of paint on a car suddenly everywhere
even in Target knickknack displays.
My cousin works in paint, the color creation industry on the chemical sales side
and he calls it an intention. There's a group
of people he works with who decide
every year what colors will trend and plaster walls,
pallets, tchotchke dorm decor.
Some call it conspiracy and hand over the tin foil to let you fold your own hat
before you share with the room the notion
that any group has any control or foreknowledge
the universe though, so often seems to line up right where we thought it might,
good or bad.
Whether that means we're in tune with divine vibration
or keen on human manipulation
aware or not, well, it can be hard to say these connections
aren't worth equal pause.

The Astronaut III

The Astronaut reaches a cluster of dust and stars somewhere near Andromeda

that's what the blue piping light on the wall says, at least.

He requests these temporary acquaintances call him Cosmonaut instead

a separate identity for distancing, disassociating with reality.

The Cosmonaut cradles another heavy glass and sinks

into the stool which swivels like a corkscrew

locking him down for a night or a day or whatever space-time

relation to the sun this place could even be

The Cosmonaut rolls an ice cube between gloved fingers

until it melts into a little stain, staying put

he wonders if he could with so little assured,

the end of the mission looming, The Cosmonaut considers

how different time ages a man so far into the solar winds

will they even recognize him back home

or has the created self become more

the Cosmonaut orders another round to see if the Astronaut can still swim.

Mind Eraser

In the days after you were gone
I collected bar stamps
on my inner wrists and hands.
I let the door men question
how long'd been since my last shower
with a smile, the scent of our embrace
buried beneath layers of ink;
to think the process cathartic,
letting those bruises rise to the surface
with an artificial substance, solace
in ginger ale fizz and your smudging
like sage, until my touch leaves prints
where I rest the glass.

I dragged a bar of rose soap, side to side,
like an over-sized pencil eraser
pressing into my skin, letting
what's left of you run thin.
Like a drawing erasing its own lines
I realized, the artist
doesn't always know what shape comes next.
These little mistakes belong to the process
of a sketch in progress, my clenched fists
around your presence here,
is no healthier than trying to drink
the black and blue circling the drain.

Does It Need A Body

Anger goes through the Empath like a wind chime.
Like the first snowfall of the year
not, a comforting tickle
shivering through bare tree limbs
down to the patio and noses
but, as in cold and quick
as in breath taken, hard to shovel through.
The Angel of Empathy does not like to think it
merely an echo of mistreatment
those footprints still on the wings, dirt clinging
to some part of his back he cannot reach,
tinnitus, inner ears still shaking
after all of these years, when
someone in the room yells
he feels it, even contained grumbling;
anger does not share its mania,
frustration does not chime a bell's song
rather, the hollow clunking of bamboo tubes
chill the Angel with dread and sorrow
to sway with the thudding
even when the wind has gone.
The Angel of Empathy longs for the silence of snow
and the great big grey to bring the solace, cushion of quiet,
the kind of quiet he wishes his own heart
would bring him.

The Sad

The sad comes whenever it wants, my door is always open,
there is a seat at the table set and ready for guests, the sad
knows this knows me knows just how I like my company
to come in without shoes and treat my home as their own
the sad almost lives here, by lease stipulations not entirely,
we put on folk songs and sing our hymns whenever we can.

I cook dinner for two though neither of us touches the food,
the sad hangs around for a nightcap and I can't send him
away, the wind coming through the door cuts the whiskey burn
on our breath and the guitar filling the room coddles him to sleep,
and I clean up the kitchen. I take a broom to the leaves blown in
take a moment with the moon to wonder when courage will pop in
for a long time no see an it's been so long, to convince me
to close the door more often, that summer will come without watching for it.

On Monday I let a wolf in the kitchen to see how much he could stomach.
I wanted to test his teeth, grapple on tile and comb the mats from his fur
we court around the dining room table a while but resolve to pleasantries
when the sad finally makes the occasion, a little late, but always on the way
I can count on the sad to pop in. The wolf howls into the bowl
tossing bits of pasta and garnish onto the placemats, handwoven
gifts from courage on my last birthday. Little things to remind me of her
every meal, every evening spent sitting at a table with rogue animals and
emotions
she calls, while the wolf and the sad debate the weather
whether or not I keep her on the line much longer won't alter
how some nights I still miss her but the desire for disaster is stronger.
The wolf will leave before Tuesday sun and the sad
will be perched on the breakfast griddle hungry and ready.

Thoracic Chamber Murmurs

Hang this stethoscope from your ears and hold the bell,
press gently into my breast and listen to the body breathe
don't move, any disturbance from shirt fabric or fingers
bawl like underwater hiccups and cloud
the beating. If you listen, close your eyes to focus,
you can hear the footsteps of my life changing direction.
There's a half step and a long stride and a jump sometimes
it's a thump glug rhythm uniquely mine and desperate
dragging in and out, waves of offices and opinions only
you can hear it, right here with me, with this binaural
halo, android jaw line, this is the closest anyone can get
to seeing the future through the dark veil of eyelids.
To sway through the palpitations, is easy, to confront them,
I'd do this myself, but the tremors
through my fingers interrupt the listening, but I'm trying
to memorize the half steps and the long strides
so when I lay on your chest and close my eyes every night
I can find a baseline for normal, feel the soundwaves
of your voice vibrating precisely tender
up. From a small laugh into a hearty smile
and for a while I can worry less
about the co-pays and the blood tests and the nervous
desire to grow closer, without coming off desperate, and dying
to be near your heart, even when I'm not, around.

Category F

Someone across the way says something like
radical policies are going to change things
or the grid will go down, we'll all be lost
or how longsit been since you checked notifications
and she's hiding. The tornado voice inside
the thing men call crazy if it has a pussy.
Quiet is preferable. Controlled is ideal.
The Lady who speaks her mind over a beer is unhinged, absurd, problematic
so she sticks to double wild, double shots of tequila gold
what the fuck is wrong with you material
gives enough a pause for onlookers to question sincerity
for the tornado voice to be heard,
the wind train hikers report from pockets of pressure in the woods
it's in her chest just waiting for controversial topics to reveal
inching close to touchdown with a fingertip point that can tear the room down
The Lady whose lived a life in the shade of the universe we call silent
will ruin your foundation and uproot your ignorance
given five minutes
too
speak

the sky will turn green
pay attention

Radio Presence

Wanting to go home
is not a grief competition
it is staring across a frozen lake for three hours when
heart conditions are more than just an affliction of poetics in this household
and yours is pumping twice over, spasms jerking the muscle around
and that wives tail about literal tissues tearing in trauma
causing the sensation of heartbreak becomes more than a metaphor
when homesick.
You're staring over a glossy summer lake
realizing you were never taught how to talk about the present
even though everything you feel seems to have the volume cranked too loud
the only language you know for it is static.
Your crying is not dramatic its the body in panic
overwhelmed with noise it has no channel for
The lake is ever-present and empty and nobody else showed up
this year for his birthday only two since he died
you realize you were never cherished nearly as much
and your remembrance will be in old books collecting dust
visited even less than that lake.
And you find yourself laying in a field with a mascara sunscreen puddle
forming in your ears
your ankles just barely in the water's edge
the sky is hazed with wildfire smoke and sunset
if losing a best friend taught you anything it's the weight of silence
shouldn't be tossed around so carelessly.
You have found the words late so many times before

There is still time to learn

which way to turn the dials

growing up an only child comes with the corporeal curse

of isolation as a means for feeling normal

everybody wants to go home

sometimes

it's ok to feel lonely at heart

from the independence your wavelength transmits on.

Take my Word

I have nerve damage
from an autoimmune disease
that went undiagnosed
for a considerable period of time.
The first attempt at identification happened
in 2011 after an undetermined trigger
had me hospital bed bound in a city I'd hardly lived in
one month into college.
Six years later I can't walk in the morning

without fireworks sparkling up my legs
and ash grinding through my hands.
It took six more doctors to figure out
the peripheral neuropathy a side effect
from a disease
and not in my head.
An unfortunate side effect of
I'm not sure what

that we accuse each other of making things up
so quickly.
When did, 'really?' become the first line treatment for
someone overcoming the fear of vulnerability
are we so afraid ourselves to be tricked
that culturally as a collective somewhere along the lines the decision was made
to question
all intentions
while giving ourselves the benefit

at our worst having come from a good start

what is haywire in the head to let this double standard of care

craft every interaction.

Just once

I want to confide a situation, all its symptoms

and the steps I took to try and remedy what has still left me feeling unwell

and be met with a tender voice that agrees things are not as they should be

understands my perspective as valid even when askew by emotions

a voice that listens to understand

not to raise doubts

The Salutatorian's Escape

There are trains and busses and men in black polos ushering queues around silk
roping.
There's marble tiled up the walls and around pillars and across the station from
corner to corner

it must be a chore to polish.

There's a ticket window with a woman behind a wooden shutter typing on a
computer
she hands the graduate a piece of paper to add to his scrapbook clippings
he sits on an ice cream scoop of a bench that stretches almost as far as the
marble

there is another man on it sleeping. The squeak of a rubber nose
in the graduate's pocket
compressed from his collapse does not seem to disturb anyone,
though it echoes around the cathedral of a building

up into the foyer and down the staircases into the subway system.
It was his comfort, his constant.

The nose was ol reliable, a child's sleeping blanket, the only thing he still owned
that could restore a sense of calm in the chaos of unknown and threat,
the stage was the only space the former clown had ever felt comfort.
It was behind him, now.

The graduate is headed out and away and into the nothingness of that first step
past completion
He's given up on speaking, on telephone conversations
at least until the wheels halt and hurl him off into a home in the making
another new city with a different climate and an internal map to-be
somewhere in those soon learned streets will be an opportunity, a reason to be
something other than second best and dancing for validation.

The man to the side rag doll snoring in the scoop of the bench stirrs some
the former clown picks at a speck of face paint he missed when washing it all
off this morning,
leaving for good blindly on a locomotive felt like a waste of drama if he didn't
change everything with it
he shaved his head down to an appropriate adult length and left all the paints in
the garbage
on the floor in a banana yellow backpack, all the graduate brought with him
were two shirts, two pants, some socks and undergarments
enough to get started, to carry him from couch to couch
and a nose
he had a laptop and notebook but wiped both out clean and fresh
squeals from the first train starting up it's hydraulics leaked in under the doors

a security guard pacing beside the ticket window leaned in to chat up the ticket
woman
The graduate reached in his pocket, and fiddled fingers over the rubber red
round
like a stress ball or simply the last scrap of an identity loved and let go, he
squeezed
until it was empty of air.

When the ragdoll man beside him jumped from a dream to join him there, he
let go
the scream of the little ball echoed louder than before and challenged the
hydraulics coming under the door

the graduate closed his eyes and sank into the expansion of it, the rubber
refilling his pocket the sound refilling his shallow nervous breathing
the room all turns to stare, and the security guard leans into the dispatch.

The puppet man scooted over, and over again twice over

until the graduate lifted an eyebrow, a cheek muscle, a half-smile and a head
nod hello
his chin buckled into folds of neck and hem line
his new neighbor returned the gesture then matched his posture, sunken into
the scoop.

They both could have asked, and equally considered
'what are you doing here' but instead
the graduate sighed, and the limp man grumbled
'me too kid, us all actually.'
A green backlit ticker above them came to a glow, the time of their departure
now approaching

the graduate fished the ticket from his other pocket and confirmed the match
the limp man sighed as he just had. The former clown looked to him and asked

'what did you say?' a sort of apology for being self-indulged on getting away
rather than being friendly.

'Do me a favor' the limp man said, reaching out a hand, 'tell me what time this ticket says and the status.'

The graduate hesitated. Having resolved to isolation
in preparation for moving on, the interaction felt foreign, dangerous even
like flecks of face paint still stuck to his tongue. 'Your bus is in seating; it
departs in a few minutes.'

And like the shock of the hydraulics or the squeal of the crushed nose ran
through the limp man a jolt
he was up to his feet and collecting himself and thanking the former clown for
the help.

They exchanged the ticket back, and the graduate sunk lower into the bench's
trench
but opened an eye a moment later to the strange man reproaching him
'give me you hand' he ushered glancing over his shoulder to the guard
the former clown raised both eyebrows and cautiously complied
like a marionette on tangled strings the strange man rustled through pockets
then presented a ring
he slid it onto the graduates finger and asked if he approved of the silver
frazzled with delight that it fit, the graduate looked uncertain and said,

'sure but man your bus is about to depart, you should probably get on it.'

New feet shuffled in the doors from the arrival, new squeals echoed across the
marble tiles
up the foyer and down the staircase, the acoustics of the place made it hard to
communicate

but the strange man humbly bowed before the former clown, put his hands together

and he stepped back. Before running to catch his ride he left the graduate with the gift,

telling him, 'in all my travels, I've never been treated
like this. As no threat. For you. A thank you.
my one good deed into the universe. Just don't tell your girlfriend

I don't want any trouble!' and the clown sat laughing as his new friend
was swallowed by the chaos of coming and going riders

a moment later the guard approached and asked the graduate if he was being bothered
the graduate said no, and pulled the red nose from his pocket, collapsing the crowned finger over it
flattening the old obsessive fixation into the center of his palm.

he said 'wait' before the guard could get far
asked a favor,
tossed the nose up, said
'can you take this rubbish to the garbage while you're up?'
he didn't need it anymore.

A Warm Thing To Hold

is how to enjoy the cider days before the wind becomes white.
with heavy breathing and homestead dreaming
it tickles me to chills every season.
between the crunching echo of walking along
and the sweets and gourds and harvested smiles;
how God never wanted a child, let alone all of us.
Gaia rolls over however many feet under sinks a broken heart
we weren't made in the image of season trends and shopping ads
we weren't meant for
what we've done with all's been given to us
a creator only wants for their creation to exist
autonomous consciousness is the sin
we give first to anything we let go of

nothing stays or holds

Save Me, Geena

If the body were a pliable dough like that at the hand of a child,
well, it was for a while. Now all these years later
it's simply a bit less corporeally malleable
all the spaces sent through and moments made memorable since infancy
through adolescence through whatever the fuck this is
I suppose there's no mental nor emotional difference in how it all shapes us,
well, these days there's something of a diver's bodysuit protecting
the skin from the water
holding the folds and weird lumps of poor choices and growths inside
something presentable
I don't wonder if our human suits showed our souls reparations
if we'd be anything attractive,
well, there is something appealing to be admired
in the smile of a survivor sure
but the way these long hands are aging
triple fold the rest of me
I am sure has much to do
with all the words penned and typed and signed across from me to you
it's just a pause. To see a child run without regard
let their voice flow wild
and wonder how long it's been
since truly having that freedom,
even as a no-holds
something type individual.
If the body in quarter-age were still so supple
could these security checkpoints and long highway rides
be other than interludes

what is all this voyage doing

to a body never designed to teleport

short of risking cross contamination with a fly

well, a mind at least

What Happens

A Cosmonaut
A Clown
and A Hopeless Romantic walk into a bar.

it's a set up you've heard before, sure.
but what do they all have in common?
Is it the state they're in, the hopelessness or the denial
to take that first step and ask why are we always coming back
to this bar, what is it about this familiar
space this communal start
that's hooked us all deeper than the poisons we pick

put a pack of nicotine gum or smokes across a table
and stare at it until your skin bubbles
order a latte but don't sip it until the foam curdles.
order a drink for the deceased
make the bartender dispose of it when you've gone
what are we doing to ourselves with little promises of feel-good
edging towards the drug of choice that stretches the void
until it is all that we know

take a gambler shopping and watch how they methodically clip coupons
it's the mental games, the telling ourselves we're doing better
by choosing the lesser
despite tormenting our body by intoxication or by withholding
something is always a little off in the stomach, a little twisted in the gut

three unsuspecting characters walk

onto a recycled stage crafted in our mind and the punchline never comes

their lives carry on as strangers making conversation in a line of seating-for-one

none of them acknowledge they're just trying to do their best

none of them acknowledge that they don't know how

this happens